The Berenstain Bears®
ON THE ROAD

Stan & Jan Berenstain

GT
PUBLISHING

The Bear family had a brand-new car. And what better way to break in a brand-new car than a big road trip!

The Bear family's new car was red like their old one. But it was a bright shiny red.

It was a convertible like their old one.
But it had a push-button top. You just
pushed a button and the top went down.

"And just smell the new-car smell!" said Papa as the members of the Bear family buckled up for safety.

"Mmm!" said the Bears as they smelled that wonderful new-car smell.

"Where are we going on our big car trip?" asked Sister.

"We are going to sample the wonderful sights of Bear Country," said Papa as he turned onto the main highway.

The first sight they sampled was the
back end of a big six-wheeler truck.

They also sampled the roar
of its engine and the smell of its
belching black exhaust.

"*Yugh!*" shouted the
Bears. But new cars have
peppy motors. So Papa
waited until it was safe and
zoomed past the six-wheeler.

The next sight they saw was a trooper hiding in the bushes. "Better slow down, Papa," said Mama. "This new car of ours not only has that new-car smell, it has a very peppy motor and it wouldn't do to get a ticket for speeding."

Papa slowed down. Brother
and Sister waved to the trooper as
they went past.

POLICE

The next sight they saw was a
great sight indeed. The whole Bear
Country valley lay before them.

There was also a sign that said: DON'T MISS GREAT GRIZZLY NATIONAL PARK — 20 MILES AHEAD.

"Look, Papa!" said Brother. "That sign says we shouldn't miss Great Grizzly National Park!"

"We're not going to miss it," said Papa, "because that's where we're headed."

The Bear family's new car was not only bright red, had a push-button top, and a peppy motor, it had drink holders.

"Look!" said Brother. "There's a drink stand! Let's get drinks so we can try out the drink holders!"

BURPSIES
COLD DRINKS

ORD
HE

The drink holders worked fine until
they went over a big bump and some
Burpsie Cola got spilled in the new car.

The next sight they saw was Point Lookout.
It was a famous beauty spot with a lovely view.
"Why are we stopping?" asked Sister.
"Because your papa and I stopped here
on our honeymoon," said Mama.

The view was very beautiful and Mama and Papa held hands as they enjoyed it.

"Where were *we* when they stopped here before?" asked Sister.

"We weren't born yet, silly," said Brother. "They were on their honeymoon!"

"Oh," said Sister.

Soon they were on their way again.
"Look!" said Brother. "An ice-
cream stand!"
"May we have ice cream?" said
Sister. "May we? May we? Please!"

ICE
CREAM

"Yum!" said the cubs as they licked their cones in the back of the car. The day was warm. So some of the ice cream dripped onto the seat. Some strawberry and some chocolate.

NOW ENTERING
GREAT GRIZZLY NATIONAL PARK

After a while they reached Great Grizzly National Park. It was a pretty long car trip. But it was worth it. There were many sights to see. There were statues of General Robert E. Grizzly and General Ulysses S. Bruin. They had been generals in the Great Bear War.

There was the famous tree under which they signed the peace treaty. Best of all was Mount Grizzmore. It was a huge mountain with the great figures of Bear Country history carved in its side.

But it had been a long day
and it was time to start for home.
Before leaving, they stopped at
the park shop, where they bought
some souvenirs, and some apples
and peanut butter crackers to eat
on the way.

PARK SHOP SNAC

The trip home was fine. Some apple cores fell behind the seats of the new car. And Sister got carsick and threw up a little. But except for that, the Bear family's big car trip had been a great success.

Of course, they were pretty tired when they finally pulled to a stop in front of the big tree house. They were almost too tired to get out of the car.

"I wonder," said Papa as he sat there, "whatever happened to that new-car smell."